Y0-BCW-368

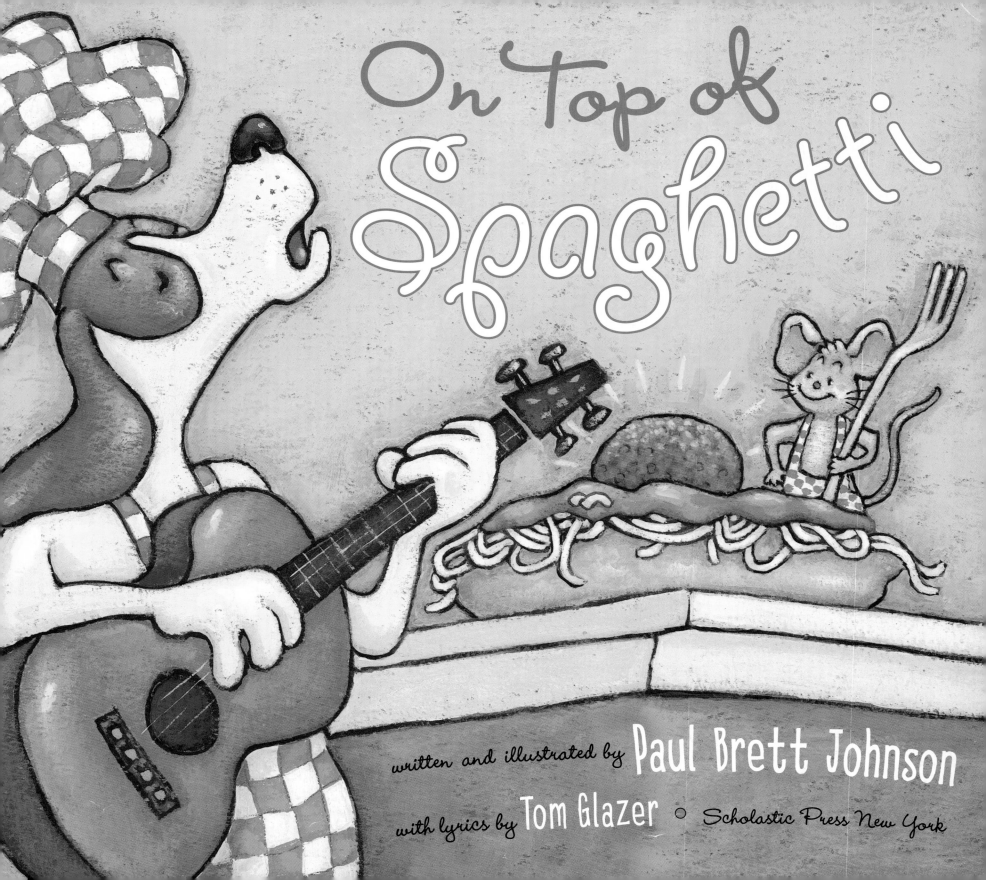

On Top of Spaghetti

written and illustrated by **Paul Brett Johnson**

with lyrics by **Tom Glazer** ○ Scholastic Press New York

Howdy, folks.

Welcome to Yodeler Jones's Spaghetti
Emporium & Musicale.
    You're just in time to hear about
the BIG SNEEZE.

It all started when they put in that fried fritter fricassee parlor next door. I couldn't haul in a customer with a line and pole.

"Yodeler," I said to myself, "it's time to upgrade the menu."

So I set out to invent the most dee-licious meatball this side of Sicily. And I likely did, but the blasted thing didn't stick around long enough for a taste test.

"On top of spaghetti

All covered with cheese,

I lost my poor meatball

When somebody...

"It rolled off the table
And onto the floor,

For all I knew, my entire future depended on that runaway meatball. I had to have a bite.

I was hot on the trail
when it flew to the Piggly Wiggly
and hit dear Miss Jenkins smack-dab in the squash.
   "Pardon my meatball," I said. Then I told my tale.

"On top of spaghetti all covered with cheese,

I lost my poor meatball when somebody sneezed."

That wasn't the end of it, though, not by a monkey's tail. My meatball went a-whooshin' and a-whizzin', and this time it landed in front of the sheriff's office.

"Pardon my meatball," I said.

"On top of spaghetti
All covered with cheese,
I lost my poor meatball
When somebody sneezed."

Next thing I knew, my meatball zinged all the way to the ballpark. By the time I caught up, some tadwhacker was just about to chomp down.

"Pardon my meatball!" I said.

That meatball shot to the outfield, boomeranged,
whizzed by shortstop, flew over the pitcher's mound,
and headed di-rectly for home plate. Bad Bubba Junior
was up at bat.

Talk about your home run! My meatball zoomed through the wild, blue yonder. And where do you reckon it landed?

"Yodeler," I said, "you might as well put up a 'For Sale' sign."
 Then lo and behold, a miracle occurred.

"The mush was as tasty
As tasty could be,
And by the next day
It grew into a tree.

"The tree was all covered
With beautiful moss,
It grew great big meatballs
And tomato sauce."

Know what? Those were the most dee-licious meatballs this side of Sicily. Nowadays, plenty of folks stop in for a bellyful. I always tell 'em, though:

"If you eat spaghetti

All covered with cheese,

Hold on to your meatball

And don't ever...

On Top of Spaghetti

Lyrics by Tom Glazer

On top of spa - ghet - ti____ All cov - ered with cheese,

I lost my poor meat - ball____ When some - bod - y SNEEZED!!!

It rolled off the table
And onto the floor,
And then my poor meatball
Rolled out of the door.

It rolled in the garden
And under a bush,
And then my poor meatball
Was nothing but mush.

The mush was as tasty
As tasty could be,
And early next summer
It grew into a tree.

The tree was all covered
With beautiful moss,
It grew great big meatballs
And tomato sauce.

So if you eat spaghetti
All covered with cheese,
Hold on to your meatball
And don't ever sneeze!

Published by Scholastic Press, an imprint of Scholastic Inc.,

Publishers since 1920. SCHOLASTIC, SCHOLASTIC PRESS, and associated logos are trademarks and/or registered trademarks of Scholastic Inc.

Library of Congress Cataloging-in-Publication Data

On top of spaghetti / story and pictures by Paul Brett Johnson; lyrics by Tom Glazer.—1st ed. p. cm.

Summary: In an adaptation of the original parody, the hound Yodeler Jones tells what happened when his beloved meatball escaped from a plateful of spaghetti and ended up under a bush outside his restaurant.

[1. Meatballs—Fiction. 2. Humorous stories.] I. Glazer, Tom. II. Title. PZ7.J63540nat 2006 [E]—dc22 2005014311 Printed in Singapore 46 First edition, May 2006 ISBN 978-0-439-74944-2 (hardcover)

The display type was set in Giddyup and Wendy. The text type was set in Eatwell Skinny and Eatwell Chubby. Book design by Richard Amari